All Joseph Wanted

All Joseph Wanted

Ruth Yaffe Radin
Illustrated by Deborah Kogan Ray

Macmillan Publishing Company
New York

Maxwell Macmillan Canada
Toronto

Maxwell Macmillan International
New York   Oxford   Singapore   Sydney

Macmillan Publishing Company is part of the
Maxwell Communication Group of Companies.

Macmillan Publishing Company
866 Third Avenue
New York, NY 10022

Maxwell Macmillan Canada, Inc.
1200 Eglinton Avenue East
Suite 200
Don Mills, Ontario M3C 3N1

First edition
Printed in the United States of America
10 9 8 7 6 5 4 3 2 1
The text of this book is set in 13 point Bembo.
Book design by Tania Garcia
The illustrations are rendered in pencil.

Library of Congress Cataloging-in-Publication Data

Radin, Ruth Yaffe.
All Joseph wanted / Ruth Yaffe Radin ; illustrated by Deborah Kogan Ray.
— 1st ed.
p.   cm.
Summary: Eleven-year-old Joseph deeply wishes that his mother
could learn how to read, since her inability to do so has complicated
their life considerably and placed a great burden on Joseph.
ISBN 0-02-775641-6
[1. Literacy—Fiction.   2. Mothers and sons—Fiction.]   I. Ray,
Deborah Kogan, ill.   II. Title.
PZ7.R1216A1   1991   [Fic]—dc20   91-12643

For my sister Mimi

One

As soon as he got outside the school building, Joseph unbuttoned his shirt all the way. Summer vacation should have been longer, he thought, looking across the street at the college kids going back and forth. At least they got to walk outdoors between classes. He had watched them during the day from the window of his sixth-grade classroom. Did they really read all those books they carried, he wondered. He was glad he didn't have any homework tonight.

Just then he felt a slap on his back. It was Mark.

"Why didn't you wait for me? All I had to do was straighten the desks."

"It was too hot in there," Joseph said. "I just wanted to get out."

"Do you want to run awhile? Soccer starts tomorrow and we have to get in shape."

"Is that what your father said?"

"He may be the coach, but I know what to do, too," Mark said.

"Okay, okay, I'll run. But I want something to eat first. I'm starved."

"You can't eat before you run. You'll get cramps."

Joseph started jogging toward the corner. "I should never have let you talk me into signing up for soccer."

Mark caught up with him. "Why?"

Joseph smiled. "I like to eat."

"We can make a loop going down Hillside, across Fourth, and up Whitney," Mark said. "Then we'll end up at my house and we can pig out."

"I'm not going uphill at the end. What about up Hillside, across Seventh, and down Whitney?"

"That's better."

The boys crossed the street and ran up the hill at the edge of campus. The campus looked like a park, except for the great stone buildings that sat there like castles.

"Are you going to go to college here some day?" Joseph asked.

"I don't know. That's a long time from now."

"You said it would be free for you because your dad teaches here."

"Faculty kids don't have to pay for classes, but they can't live on campus free."

The hill was steep enough and long enough to make talking hard after that. When they reached the corner of Seventh Street, Mark stumbled onto the grass of the campus and lay down on his back. "I've got to take a break."

Joseph sat down next to him, breathing hard. "Your face is really red."

Mark looked at him. "How come yours isn't?"

"I come up the hill to school every day, remember? And I usually run so I won't be late. All you have to do is walk across on a flat street."

The boys looked toward the river, with the two bridges crossing it, at the foot of the hill. The people who lived down there near Joseph worked in the factories along the river and shopped at the small stores on Fourth Street. Most of them lived in row houses, built one after another, many on streets that hugged the steep slope going up from Fourth.

Joseph stood up. "Come on, let's go. I want to get to your house so I can call home. My mother really worries if I'm not back when she thinks I should be."

They started running along Seventh Street. That far up the hill, the houses were bigger and separated from one another. The people who lived in them often had something to do with the college.

When the boys reached Mark's house, they heard music coming through the open windows and the front door, which was half open. It was a Dutch door, so the top half could be open while the bottom half stayed closed. Mark had said that door was the reason they had bought the house. His mother was Dutch, and it reminded her of home.

Mark's mother was on the living room floor doing leg lifts when they walked in. She smiled at them while she counted, "Four, three, two, one." Then she stood up and wiped her forehead with a towel. "I had meetings all morning, so I had to put off the workout.

Are you two set for soccer tomorrow?"

"We just ran up Hillside, along Seventh, and down," Mark said.

"Good. Do you have soccer shoes, Joseph?" she asked.

"I was going to wear sneakers."

"We should have something around here that Mark's brother has outgrown. They'd be in the storage closet. Come on. We'll look now."

"I have to call home first, or my mother will worry," Joseph said, following her.

"Of course. You know where the phone is."

Joseph was used to Mark's house now, but the first time he was there, it had seemed like a mansion. Just inside the front door was something Mark called a foyer. There were great openings with wooden columns on each side between the two living rooms. Beyond them was a dining room. There were books everywhere, and where there weren't any bookshelves, there were pictures on the walls. Upstairs, Mark and his brother had their own bedrooms.

After Joseph punched his number on the wall phone in the kitchen, he watched Mark's mother look through the closet in the hall. He knew all kinds of sports things were kept there: wet suits for wind surfing and surf boarding, hockey sticks and pucks, ice skates, and balls for soccer and baseball. It was almost like a sports shop. The ski equipment was in the basement.

The phone rang four times before his mother answered. He turned his back to the hall. "I'm at Mark's," he said.

"I was worried. You're usually here by now. When will you be home?"

Joseph looked at the clock. It was four. "Could I stay another hour?"

He heard his five-year-old brother, Peter, whining as his mother answered, "Don't be any later. I need your help."

Joseph hung up, knowing what kind of help she needed. He was glad to be distracted by Mark's mother, who came into the kitchen then. She had two pairs of soccer shoes for him to try on, and shin guards, too.

"I'm putting pizza in the oven, okay?" Mark said, opening the freezer door.

"Okay."

"Then I want to show you my new cards."

"Who did you get?" Joseph tried on one shoe.

"The Kid."

"Ken Griffey, Jr.?"

"You said it. How would you like a candy bar named after you? I got a Bo Jackson rookie card and a Will the Thrill one, too."

"Will Clark! How much did that one cost?"

"My uncle gave it to me."

Joseph tied the second shoe and stood up. They felt pretty good. He didn't have any relatives who could give him baseball cards. He had started collecting, too, but bought all of them with his own money. Maybe the three-cent cards he bought would be worth a lot someday. He wished he had a Bo Jackson. That man was something else—a running back in pro football and an outfielder in the majors.

"Try the other pair," Mark's mother said. "Then decide."

The second pair was even better. At first it had bothered Joseph to take things from Mark's family. But then they had convinced him that he was doing them a favor by using what they couldn't use anymore. Still, no matter how much Joseph took, he didn't think their house would ever be uncluttered.

After the boys had eaten, they went up to Mark's room. When Joseph checked the time again, it was already 4:45. "I have to go. Should I come over about nine tomorrow morning?"

"Maybe a little earlier, since it's the first day. Don't forget the cleats and shin guards."

"Why don't I just leave them here since you're taking me?"

"Good idea."

Joseph ran down Whitney Street to Fourth and then walked along Fourth, looking in the store windows. There were lots of college kids hanging out in the shop that sold used CDs and tapes. He walked past the Chinese restaurant, which was mostly empty, and the Boys Club. Across the street was the library. He usually went there with Mark, but because Mark had been in the Netherlands all summer visiting his grandparents and other relatives of his mother's, Joseph hadn't borrowed books since June.

He turned right onto Iron Street, walking to the end of a stone building that was two stories high in the front and only one story high in the back. His apartment was in that building, above a meeting hall.

Joseph ran up the fire escape and stepped through a gate onto a flat roof with sides around it high enough to make it safe. His sister Jen was playing there with her friend, and he started to walk past them to the kitchen door without saying anything.

"Peter's sick," Jen said. "Mommy took him to the clinic this afternoon."

Joseph stopped. "What's wrong?"

"I don't know. He's got to take medicine."

Joseph went inside and walked through the kitchen to the front room. His mother was holding his little brother on her lap. He was sleeping, and when she saw Joseph, she put the child gently on the sofa and got up.

"I took him to the clinic and they gave me medicine for him." She got the bottle from the kitchen counter and handed it to Joseph. "What do the labels say? All the doctor said was that Peter should have it every six hours around the clock."

Joseph took the bottle from his mother. "Besides that, it says, 'Shake well before using.

Keep in refrigerator. Do not freeze. Finish all medication unless otherwise prescribed by doctor.' "

Joseph's mother took the bottle and looked at it, then at Joseph. "The words were too hard for Jen," she said.

He wished his sister were old enough to help. But she was just seven. It would be a while before she could. If only his mother could read. That was all Joseph wanted.

Two

Almost three weeks of school had passed. The mornings were cool enough so that when Joseph woke up he pulled the covers close around his chin. He looked out the window next to his bed and saw the top leaves of the maple tree beginning to turn yellow. Soon enough they would start to fall. He looked toward Peter's bed. It was empty.

Everyone else in the family was probably in the kitchen already. Breakfast was the only time they were all together. His father had two jobs, one as a night watchman, and he would just have gotten home. After eating a little, he would go to sleep till he was due to work the three-to-eleven shift at the plant.

Joseph got up and walked around Peter's bed to their dresser. He opened the top drawer, where his shirts were stacked, neatly folded. His mother never asked him to help with his clothes. She hadn't said so, but Joseph knew it was because he was the one who had to help her most with reading. His father was either working or sleeping.

Joseph had asked his mother once why she'd never learned. "You went to school," he had said.

She had shrugged her shoulders. "We moved a lot. Sometimes I didn't have nice clothes to wear, so I didn't go."

One time when he'd been mad he had said, "Grown-ups are supposed to know how to read."

His mother had turned away from him, and he'd heard her crying quietly. He would never forget that he had made her cry.

She could do lots of things. Joseph knew she was smart, and she took good care of them. She was just twenty-seven and was the prettiest mother he had ever seen. Maybe if he hadn't been born so soon, she would have finished school and learned to read, he thought. But his father hadn't finished, and he knew how. Still,

Joseph would help her and not complain. He wouldn't let anyone else know about her problem, either.

Joseph took out his clothes and dressed quickly, smelling hot cereal and toast. As he started to put his books into his book bag, he saw the sealed letter addressed to his parents still inside it. His teacher, Mrs. Novak, had given the same letter to seven other kids in his class. "Have your parents read it and we'll talk about it tomorrow," she had said. "Don't worry. You haven't done anything wrong." He'd show the letter to his father now.

When Joseph went into the kitchen, everyone was at the table. He handed the envelope to his father. "Mrs. Novak said it's nothing bad. Some other kids got one, too."

"There's oatmeal in the pot for you," his mother said.

He took his bowl to the stove and helped himself.

Joseph's father read the typewritten letter to himself and then looked at Joseph's mother. "They're asking us to let Joseph be part of a special program."

"What kind? "

Joseph listened.

"It's called Target. It's for kids they think have a lot of ability but need—what's the word they use?" Joseph's father looked back at the letter. "Enrichment, that's what they call it."

Joseph's mother looked worried. "It could be too hard. Maybe there would be a lot of extra work to do."

Joseph reached for the letter. "Let me read it." He looked at it quickly. "At the end it says you have to go to a meeting."

His mother looked at Jen. "I'll do your hair now. Go get the ties." Then she turned to Peter, who was still eating. "Finish up. It's almost time to go."

"When's the meeting?" Joseph's father asked.

"Seven next Tuesday night. But if you can't go to the meeting, you can talk to the teacher after school any day next week."

"I can't go at either time. Let me see that letter." Joseph's father read it to himself again. "It says a parent has to be there so the teacher can explain what it's all about." He looked at Joseph. "Mommy can go."

Joseph looked at his mother fixing Jen's hair. She had never gone to anything at school.

"Maybe you can just sign something that says we give permission if you think he should do it," she said to Joseph's father.

"Why do I have to take care of everything?" He stood up and started to say something more, but stopped short. "I'm tired. I'm going to sleep."

Joseph took the open note and folded it, putting it back into the envelope. "I'll find out more about it today."

"Hurry up, Peter," Jen said. "We have to go soon."

At least he didn't have to walk his little brother to school, Joseph thought. When he was ready, he got his book bag and started toward the door.

"Did you brush your teeth?" his mother asked quietly.

Joseph turned around. She seemed so small, sitting at the empty table. He went over to her and opened his mouth extra wide. "See?"

They both laughed, and he hugged her goodbye.

During reading, Mrs. Novak talked with Joseph's group about the Target program.

"Once a week you'd have a different experience during language arts," she said. "You'd visit places in the neighborhood to listen to people talk about their jobs."

"You mean we'd have field trips every week?" one of the kids said.

"I guess you could call them that. But sometimes people would come here to talk to you, or you might interview someone who works in this school instead."

"What will the other kids do while we do that?" Joseph asked.

"They'll do regular school assignments with me and their other teachers," Mrs. Novak said. "You'll be with professors and their students from the college. The idea behind this special program is to see if all the experiences you'll have, along with more reading and writing, will help you adjust to the work in middle school. You might get some good ideas, too, about what you want to be when you grow up."

"Will we have to do a lot extra for Target?"

Mrs. Novak smiled. "No more than you can handle." Then she said, "How many of your parents are coming to the meeting Tuesday night?"

Six kids raised their hands. Joseph put his halfway up.

"Is your hand up or not, Joseph?"

"I'm not sure if my mother can come. I know my father can't any time."

"If your mother can't come Tuesday night, we'll set up a daytime appointment. I want to show all your parents some of your work and tell them about the program. They'll have to sign some forms giving us permission to include you."

Joseph panicked. His mother wouldn't be able to read the forms or any of the papers Mrs. Novak would show her. She could sign her name. That was about all.

"Are we allowed to come to the meeting, too?" he asked.

"I see no reason why not."

"She may still want to talk it over with my father. Could she take the forms home?"

Mrs. Novak smiled. "Joseph, don't worry so much. Target is a wonderful opportunity."

For the rest of the day, Joseph did worry. At lunch he hardly talked to Mark.

"What's wrong with you?"

"Huh?"

"What's wrong with you? You've hardly said anything. School spaghetti isn't that good."

Joseph wasn't about to tell Mark that his mother couldn't read. Instead he said, "I was thinking about that Target program."

"I heard Mrs. Novak talk to your group about it."

"It's for the poor kids," Joseph said. "Nobody from your neighborhood is in it, just the ones from mine who don't have expensive baseball cards and closets full of sports stuff."

"Why are you getting mad?" Mark said. "I can't help it if we have that stuff. And I don't care what you have or don't have. That Target program sounds good. You'll get out of school all the time to go meet people. I wish I could be in it."

"You're too rich."

"Yeah. I'm so rich I have to pay my own $2.30 library fine today after school."

"I'll walk there with you," Joseph said quietly.

Three

For the next couple of days, Mrs. Novak had Joseph's reading group put together folders for their parents to see. It was like getting ready for parent-teachers' conferences, Joseph thought, only it was too early for the regular ones, and just eight kids in the class were doing it. He was going to go to the Tuesday night meeting with his mother. He'd tell her ahead of time what would be in the folder and what she'd have to know.

Even though he'd told her the plan, she was worried. "Maybe you'll be able to whisper what I'm supposed to be reading, Joseph, while we're at the meeting. But you have to make sure nobody hears, or people will think I need you to read for me."

"But you do." As soon as he had said that, Joseph had known it was a mistake.

His mother had looked down. "You're right. I just cause a lot of trouble."

"We'll sit in back or off to one side," he had said. "I don't mind." But inside he had known he really did.

Joseph looked at the standardized test scores in the folder from last year in fifth grade. The only thing he could figure out was that X's toward the right side of the chart were better than X's toward the left. He did best in math and science and worst in language arts, which Mrs. Novak said were writing skills. Maybe that's why he didn't like to write much. He'd add some of the words that were on the test sheet to the list he was making for his mother. If she could learn them before the meeting, she might understand more of what Mrs. Novak was talking about.

Joseph took the list from his desk. Then he wrote: *language arts, mathematics, science,* and *social studies.* His mother could read the numbers that showed the scores for each one, and she'd be able to understand the X's, too. Joseph folded the list and put it into his pocket. It was Friday, so there would be time over the weekend for him to help her. Maybe his father could, too, Joseph thought. Then he changed his mind. All Joseph's father did on his days off was watch sports on TV. He said he was too tired for anything else.

After school Joseph ran with Mark. They had been running every day since soccer started. Joseph had talked Jen into taking his book bag home, and Mark dropped his off at his father's office on campus.

It was getting easier, and instead of going up the hill, then across, they kept going till they got to Mountain Park. Then they ran along the path to North Lookout. From there they could see the whole valley.

Mark peeled a little bark from a nearby sassafras tree and gave Joseph a piece of it to chew. They sat down on the dry grass, tasting the flavor of soda from the bark and feeling the fall wind in their faces. The air was clear, even though smoke was coming from some of the factory chimneys. Maybe it was just steam, Joseph thought. His father said that's what it was sometimes.

"Today I had to write about what I wanted to be when I grew up," Joseph said. "It was for the folders."

"What did you say?"

"I didn't know what to say. Mostly I thought about what I didn't want."

"Like what?"

"Like not working two jobs and sleeping during the day like my father." Joseph looked down at the river flowing through town, then winding through open farmland where the hills were gentler and wider apart, where space wasn't filled with factories and row houses. "Maybe I won't live here anymore someday. I don't want to live upstairs from a meeting hall. I want to have a yard instead of a roof."

"I like your roof," Mark said. "It's fun to sleep out on."

Joseph looked at Mark and didn't say anything.

"Don't start getting mad," Mark said. "So what did you write finally?"

"I said I wanted to be a policeman."

"Do you really?"

"I don't know, but I figured Mrs. Novak would believe me. Kids are always saying they want to be policemen or firemen. I know enough about what they do so I could write something. What difference does it make?"

Joseph tossed the sassafras bark into a bush and started to retie his sneaker laces. "Let's get going."

When Joseph got home, his mother was folding laundry. He showed her the word list right away. "I'll help you learn these. They're all on papers in my folder."

She took the list from him and looked at it. "I don't think I can do it, Joseph. You'll be there to help."

"Can't you even try?"

"I have to make supper as soon as I finish doing this. Go out and get Jen. She has to set the table tonight. Here, you take the paper."

Joseph didn't give up. "I'll read them to you."

Just then his little brother came into the kitchen, crying, and his mother turned away to see what was wrong.

Joseph went out to the roof. He heard his sister on the sidewalk below. "You have to set the table," he called down. Then he folded the paper with the list into an airplane and aimed it at her. It went into the gutter.

Jen picked it up. "You're not supposed to do

that," she yelled up at him. "I'm going to tell Mommy."

Joseph turned away from her without answering. Maybe he'd go look at his baseball cards. But as he started walking through the kitchen, his mother stopped him.

"I need you to go to the store for me, Joseph."

"For what?"

"First, canned tomatoes. There's no paper on the can and it's red with white around the top. The letters are mostly yellow and there's a picture of two tomatoes on it. Be sure to get that kind."

Joseph nodded. "What else?"

"Applesauce, the big jar with five apples across the top of the label."

He took the money and left.

The next morning when Joseph went into the kitchen, only his father was sitting at the table. Saturdays were different from the rest of the week. Joseph had just heard the shower water turn off. That was where his mother must be. His sister and brother were watching cartoons.

"I have to eat fast to get to Mark's house," he said. "We've got to leave for soccer by nine."

"Sit down, Joseph," his father said. "I want to talk to you."

"I shouldn't have shot the airplane at Jen."

"That's not what I want to talk about. It's the words on it."

"I know. Why can't Mom learn them? I was going to teach her the words so she'd know something on Tuesday night."

"She's going to the meeting, Joseph. That's hard enough. Don't put pressure on her right now."

"You got mad at her, too, when she didn't want to go."

"I was tired. Working two jobs isn't easy. It costs a lot to live now."

Just then Joseph noticed his mother standing in the kitchen door. She was in her bathrobe with her hair wrapped in a towel. He wondered what she had heard.

She walked into the kitchen. "You have to hurry, Joseph. Mark's father is nice to take you to soccer every week. You don't want to make them late."

"I know." Joseph poured dry cereal into his

bowl and started eating quickly. He couldn't wait to kick that ball and run. Today he'd control it better, not letting it get too far away from him. He'd think about passing instead of kicking blindly when he had to get rid of the ball. He was on a team. He didn't have to go it alone, the way he had to at home. Why was he the only one in the family who wanted his mother to learn how to read?

When he got to Mark's house, they were putting the mesh bags of soccer balls into the back of the van.

"Go get your cleats and shin guards," Mark said. "They're right inside the door."

Joseph ran to get them and almost bumped into Mark's mother, who was on her way out.

"I'm sorry," he said, and looked at the strange way she was dressed.

She laughed. "I'm going to New York for the day with a friend. I know it seems funny to be dressed up with sneakers on, but we'll do a lot of walking." She opened her tote bag. "See, I have nice shoes to put on when we get to the theater and the restaurant. But I want to be comfortable the rest of the time."

"How are you getting there?" Joseph asked.

"By bus. It leaves in half an hour. I have to hurry." She walked past him. "Have a good time at soccer, everybody."

Joseph watched as she got into the compact car. Then he picked up his cleats and shin guards and ran out, too. This family was so different from his.

Four

Joseph watched his mother put a barrette in her hair, then pick up a pencil to draw around her eyes. He never understood her doing that. "You look fine," he said, concerned that they'd be late and that she'd poke herself. She never had, as far as he knew.

"I'm almost ready. Would you get my jacket for me?"

"The meeting starts in twenty minutes," Joseph said. "We'll have to walk fast." At least Peter and Jen were already next door with Mrs. Rivera, he thought.

"Did you tell Mrs. Novak we want to take the forms home?"

"Yes. Don't worry." But Joseph didn't tell her *he* was worrying, not knowing exactly what was going to happen that night. Other kids would be there, too. Whatever he had to do, he'd try not to let it show that his mother couldn't read. He didn't know what had happened to the list of words, but he didn't want to mention it now for fear he would upset her. As far as he knew, she hadn't looked at it since before he had folded it into an airplane.

When they got to school, Joseph's mother reached for his hand. Joseph pulled it away. "I'm too big." Knowing she was afraid, he whispered, "All you'll have to do is sit there, I bet. Come on. We have to go to the all-purpose room."

They walked past lots of closed doors, down a hall that Joseph thought seemed longer than usual. Voices were coming from the open room at the end. When they got there, Mrs. Novak was waiting just inside. She handed Joseph's folder to his mother and smiled. "I'm so glad you were able to come tonight. I like having Joseph in my class very much." Then she said, "Why don't you sit at one of the tables and look at what's in the folder while we wait for the rest of the parents to come."

"There's an empty table on the side of the room," Joseph whispered, and led the way, saying hi to the kids they passed as they walked over to it. After they had sat down, Joseph opened the folder. "I'll try to explain things to you."

His mother nodded.

He showed her copies of tests from the year before, pointing out what he knew about the numbers.

"I understand them," she said, seeming a little bit more relaxed.

Then he showed her the paper he had written about wanting to be a policeman.

"Is that what you want to do someday, Joseph?" his mother asked.

"I don't know. But we had to write something."

By then everyone was there. Mrs. Novak introduced a professor from the college across the street. "Dr. Graybar is in the Department of Education," she began. "He has done research on the social makeup of schools and its influence on the learning environment."

Joseph didn't know exactly what that meant, but at least he had been able to talk with his mother about the things in the folder before the meeting started.

He looked at her out of the corner of his eye.

She had to be much younger than the other mothers there. Maybe she'd be able to go back to school and nobody would know she was older than the other high-school kids. But you learned to read in elementary school, he thought. She couldn't go that far back.

Joseph remembered seeing a few pictures of her when she was his age. In one she was sitting barefoot on a horse at the farm where she said her father had worked. Someone there had taken the picture and made an extra print for her.

"We didn't wear shoes much in the summer," she had said when Joseph had asked about it. He had wanted her to tell him about her mother and father, too. He didn't even call them grandma and grandpa, since he hadn't known them. All she had ever said was that she didn't have parents anymore.

The professor was talking, and Joseph's mother seemed to be listening carefully. When he was done, he asked if anybody had any questions.

It was quiet.

Then he said, "I'm going to pass out an outline of Project Target and some forms I want

you to take home. Look them over. Think about what you heard tonight. Then I hope you'll sign the forms, giving your child permission to participate in this program. Since it's not part of the regular school curriculum, you must give us a signed go-ahead."

Mrs. Novak stood up. "I'd like to add that I think all of your children have the ability to do wonderful things. Look in your child's folder."

Joseph stiffened.

"Find the paper about what your child wants to do someday."

Joseph's mother took it right out.

"How many of your children said they wanted to be policemen or nurses?"

All but one parent raised their hands.

Mrs. Novak smiled. "Project Target should give your son or daughter ideas about lots of jobs, lots of professions, by introducing him or her to people who work in different fields. It's fine to want to be a policeman or a nurse, but I think that was a goal for some because they didn't know what choices they have."

Joseph's mother smiled at him. She seemed to be having a good time, he thought.

At the end of the meeting there were refreshments, and then everyone left. It had worked, after all, Joseph thought as they walked down the hill to Fourth Street.

"What do you think of Target?" his mother asked him.

"It sounds okay. Will you have Dad sign the forms?"

"I could, if you tell me where to do it," she said quietly.

They didn't talk again till they were almost home. Then Joseph's mother said, "I think I should get a job now that you're all in school."

Joseph looked at her, surprised. "Why?"

"I can help earn money. Your father shouldn't carry the full burden. Maybe after a while he won't have to work two jobs."

She must have heard them talking at breakfast the other day. "What would you do?" Joseph asked.

"I don't know. Would you read me the help-wanted ads in the paper?"

"Sure."

Joseph looked across the street. "The drug-store is open. Maybe they have papers."

The rack was just inside the door. Joseph's mother took the paper displayed on top. Joseph looked at it and whispered, "No. It's from Philadelphia." Then he picked up the local one, and they payed for it.

Outside his mother said, "Don't say anything about my wanting to get a job."

"Why not?"

"Let's just wait, okay?"

"Do you think Dad will mind?"

"I don't know. I'll talk to him."

"When?"

"I don't know yet."

After his sister and brother had gone to bed, Joseph still had another half hour to stay up because he was the oldest. "Let's look at the paper in the kitchen," he said. "I'll read the ads to you."

Joseph started skimming. Every job seemed to require some reading. "What do you think you could do?"

"What about cooking?"

"You're good at that," Joseph said. "Here's one. 'Bakery Help Finisher, good wages, early A.M. hours. Apply in person.' What's a bakery help finisher? Putting frostings on?"

"It doesn't matter. I have to be here early in the morning to get you all off to school."

"What about 'Counter Help—full or part-time' at Kentucky Fried Chicken?"

"I need something I can walk to."

"You could be a cleaning person. 'Modern offices. Must be neat and reliable. Evening hours.' "

"Dad works evenings. I can't go out, too."

Joseph was quiet. If she worked in a grocery store, she'd need to read labels and price charts. Sometimes the cashier had to do that when he bought things. If his mother took care of kids, she'd have to read directions for giving medicine. He wouldn't be there to help. If she cleaned somebody's office or store, could she tell one cleaner from another and know how to use it without reading? He was always reading those kinds of directions to her.

Joseph looked at his mother's anxious face. If she could only read, it would be so much easier.

"Maybe I could go to an employment agency, and they could help me find a job."

"Where is there one?"

"Look in the Yellow Pages. That's what they say to do on the radio."

Joseph got the phone book and looked under

Employment. "There are a lot of them listed. Here's one on Main Street."

"That's on the other side of the river. I know how to get there, and it's close enough to walk to. What's the name of it?"

"Jobs Unlimited. It says it's open nine to five, Monday through Friday. When are you going to go?" Joseph asked.

"Maybe tomorrow."

"While we're in school?"

"Yes."

"Maybe you should tell Dad before you go."

Joseph's mother stood up. "Don't you worry about that. Isn't it time to go to bed?" She looked at the clock. "It's almost ten."

Of all things, why did she have to know how to tell time, Joseph thought.

Five

The rain came down hard, then slowed, then came down hard again, pressing the fallen leaves against buildings and clogging the sewer openings with them after they were washed along in the gutter. Joseph went from doorway to doorway on the way to school, walking under awnings whenever he could.

He was late in leaving, since it had taken time to explain to his mother about the bus. She had wanted to take one and go that day, instead of waiting and walking when the weather cleared.

"It's the one with *C* above the windshield where the sign tells where the bus goes," Joseph had said. "*C* for City Center." She knew her letters well enough, but he was worried about her taking the bus alone. She had never done that before. "It costs one dollar, and you pay when you get on."

"I know," she had said. "I've taken the bus before with all of you."

"But this time, don't get off till everyone else does at the main library. Then walk down the hill past the old stone buildings to Main Street."

"It's one forty-five Main Street. I'll remember that."

"You could wait and go after school with me," Joseph had said. "We have early dismissal today because of teachers' meetings. I forgot to tell you."

Joseph's mother hadn't wanted to leave Jen and Peter next door with Mrs. Rivera again so soon. If she went in the morning, Peter would be in school, and she'd be home in time to make dinner for Joseph's father before he went to work. And of course he would be sleeping while she was at the agency. "If I don't get a job," she had said, "Dad doesn't have to know."

Joseph looked out at a sudden downpour as he stood under the metal awning in front of the fruit market. From there on, he'd have to run. There was no shelter going up the hill, just parking lots and chain-link fences surrounding the school playground. Maybe it was all right that his mother was going alone, he thought. Usually she waited for someone to help her. Maybe going to school the night before had been a good thing. She didn't seem so frightened.

As Joseph was about to cross the street and start up the hill, a city truck pulled over to the curb along with a police car. The policeman went into the middle of the road and began directing all traffic to turn right at the intersection.

"Wait under the awning for now, young man," he said to Joseph. "I'll let you cross soon."

The city workers started putting up road blocks with detour signs pointing in the same direction that the policeman was directing traffic. A few more people walked up to the corner to cross and then waited under the awning, too.

Joseph turned to the man next to him. "What's going on?"

"The Hill-to-Hill Bridge is being closed for repairs. They're rerouting all traffic onto the Park Street Bridge. It's going to be a mess for about three months."

"Where will the bus go?" Joseph asked, pan-

icking. His mother would get mixed up.

"Instead of stopping at the library, it's going up to Broad and New streets. Then it will head back."

"How do you get to the library from there?"

Just then, the policeman motioned them to cross, and the man Joseph had been talking to headed toward the newspaper's printing plant. He waved to Joseph. "Somebody can tell you over there. Why don't you just go to the library on this side of the river? It would be easier."

Joseph waved to him and started running up the hill. He'd call home to tell his mother not to go alone on the bus. For sure she'd get lost.

When he got to school, Mrs. Novak gave him permission to use the office phone. He dialed, letting it ring long enough so that he knew his mother wasn't there, but not long enough so that his father would answer. His father had to sleep to be alert when he went to the plant in the afternoon.

Maybe his mother would just ask for directions when she got to the other side of the river, Joseph thought. And since everyone on the bus would be used to a different route, probably lots of people would ask questions.

At recess they stayed in the room because of the weather, but they could sit with a friend and play board games or just talk. Mark had brought in some baseball cards and a price guide.

"Look up Carl Yastremski, 1967," he said.

"It's probably way over a hundred dollars," Joseph said, having trouble getting interested.

Mark didn't notice. "I looked up a 1953 Mickey Mantle last night. How much do you think that card is worth? More than three thousand? More than five thousand?" Mark asked. "More than—"

"Who would be able to spend thousands on cards?" Joseph said.

"Maybe the players. I read Reggie Jackson collected them."

"Have you ever been across the river at Broad and New streets?" Joseph asked, changing the subject.

"Probably. What's there?"

"I don't know. That's where the bus stops now that the Hill-to-Hill Bridge is being fixed and they're rerouting traffic."

Joseph turned the pages of the price guide,

pretending to look things up. He wanted to tell Mark about his mother. He had to tell someone.

Maybe he'd say, "My mother has a problem and I have to help her a lot."

Mark would answer, "What kind of problem?"

He'd tell him right out. "She can't read."

"She can't read?" he'd say. "Are you kidding?"

Joseph closed the price guide. "I don't feel like looking things up anymore."

"You know what?" Mark said. "You're acting funny."

Joseph didn't answer. Maybe they couldn't really be best friends. Mark wouldn't understand. How could he? His parents might even say, "Don't spend so much time with Joseph. He isn't like us."

"Well," Mark said, "what's wrong?"

Just then Mrs. Novak told the class that recess was over.

Joseph stood up. "I'm just tired, I guess. I stayed up late." He looked out the window on his way back to his seat. It was drizzling. If she were walking, it wouldn't be too bad now. His father didn't even know what was happening today. Joseph felt so alone.

After school he ran home. On early dismissal days, he got there before his father went to work. When Joseph walked in, his father was pacing back and forth in the kitchen. His mother wasn't there, Joseph knew it.

"Do you know where she is?" his father asked. "Peter got home at twelve-thirty and woke me up. She's usually here." Then he shouted, "Where is she?" Joseph had never heard him raise his voice quite like that.

"She wanted to get a job," Joseph said, and told his father the whole story. "She was going to walk to Main Street, but because of the rain she decided to go by bus."

"Why didn't she tell me?"

"She wanted to get the job first. After I saw the detour being set up, I tried to call home when I got to school."

"I didn't hear the phone."

"I didn't let it ring long. I should have."

They both sat down. Joseph's father put his head in his hands.

Just then the back door opened. Joseph's mother was standing there. His father stood up and walked over to her. "Are you all right?"

She put her head against his chest. "Did Joseph tell you?"

"He told me. Why did you want a job?"

She pulled away from him and sat down at the kitchen table. "You work too hard. I wanted to be able to help, too."

Joseph couldn't keep quiet any longer. "Did you get lost?"

"Yes."

His father sat down.

"The bus didn't go where you said it would. When it stopped, I asked the driver how to get to Main Street and he started naming streets where I should turn. But I couldn't read the street signs. I kept asking people where to go and finally I got to the agency. It wasn't that far away."

"What happened there?" Joseph's father asked.

His mother looked down. "They wanted to give me some tests. I asked them if I had to take tests for a cooking job. They asked if I had transportation. I thought about the bus trip over there and I told them I wanted to think a little more about what I could do."

"Did you bring any forms home?" Joseph asked.

"No. They didn't give me any. They weren't interested in helping me find a job. I knew that after a few minutes." She started to cry.

Joseph's father stood up and stroked her hair. "I have to go. Don't worry. We can manage." Then he turned to Joseph. "You help your mother while I'm at work."

Joseph fought back tears. "I will."

After his father left, Joseph asked, "What took you so long getting home?"

"I was afraid to take the bus so I started to walk. But the streets I knew were blocked off. I walked around for a while, seeing if I could figure out where to go, and finally I went into a restaurant to use the ladies' room. A policeman who was eating there saw that I was upset. He came over to me and I told him what was wrong."

"You told him you were lost?"

"In a way. I told him I didn't know how to read."

"You told him that?"

"And he didn't laugh or act surprised. He said lots of people don't know how to read and that there are reading classes for grown-ups. Then he gave me a ride home."

"In a police car?" Joseph's eyes were wide open. "Did he use the police radio?"

His mother nodded and smiled.

"I wish I could ride in a police car for fun someday," Joseph said.

They both laughed. Then she reached out and took his hands. "It wasn't just for fun, Joseph, but what happened today made me want to learn to read. Will you teach me?"

"You said there are classes for grown-ups," Joseph said. "Where did the policeman say they are?"

Joseph's mother shook her head. "I couldn't go to them."

"Why not?"

"You can teach me."

He looked at her, remembering how she didn't want to learn the word list he had brought home. "I'm only in sixth grade."

"But you're so smart. Mrs. Novak says so."

Joseph pulled his hands away. If she wanted to learn, he thought, maybe he'd be able to teach her. If she did learn, then she could do things on her own, maybe even get a job so his father wouldn't have to work so hard.

"I'll try," Joseph said.

Six

After three weeks, Joseph had taught his mother the sounds for the first six letters of the alphabet. They had even made words from them. At first it had been fun when his mother had written sentences with just those few letters and *I*. She had written, "I fed dad."

"That's good," Joseph had said. "Put a capital letter at the beginning of *Dad*." Then he had taught her *is*.

She had written, "Dad is bad." They'd both laughed. He had taught her *the*, and then he had taught her to put a capital letter at the beginning of a sentence. She had written, "The bed is bad" and "I fed the cab." They had laughed some more.

When he'd said, "I know a word you should learn—*detour*," she had nodded.

"I won't ever forget that one," she'd said,

and had written it three times.

But now Joseph wondered what would happen after they'd gone through the whole alphabet. His sister and brother were in bed, and Joseph and his mother were sitting at the kitchen table. His mother opened the spiral notebook she used for writing, ready for the lesson.

He had to say something. "I don't know if I'm teaching you the right way."

"But I'm learning, aren't I?"

"I guess so. But we need books. In school the teacher uses books and workbooks. She doesn't make everything up."

"I should have thought of that," his mother said. "There are simple books at the library, aren't there?"

Joseph wished he had the nerve to say that he didn't want to teach her, not just that he wasn't sure he was doing it right. Project Target was taking a lot of time. It was sort of fun visiting places in the neighborhood, but he had to do a lot of extra reading and writing.

"Where are the classes," he asked her, "for teaching grown-ups to read?"

"At the library."

"Here or across the river?"

"Here," she said quietly.

"What?" Joseph shouted.

His mother put her finger to her lips. "You'll wake Peter and Jen." Then she put her hands on her lap and whispered, "Don't you want to help me, Joseph?"

"It's so close. Why don't you want to go?"

"I'm afraid I won't be able to learn there."

"Why?"

"Because I couldn't learn before when I went to school."

"I'm going to find out about the classes," Joseph said.

"When you're at the library, will you pick out some books for me?" his mother said. "Then maybe it will be easier for you to teach me."

Joseph got up from the table. He didn't want to teach his mother anymore. Why couldn't he just say that? Instead he said, "I'll go to the library after school tomorrow." Ever since he had started teaching his mother to read, he had stopped running with Mark, so what difference did it make? It had gotten hard to talk to Mark when all Joseph could think about was not saying anything about his mother's problem.

The next day, as Joseph walked down the hill after school, he looked past the buildings to the river. He wished he could go straight to its banks and skip stones. Instead, he turned onto Fourth Street. He'd find out about the adult reading class and look for easy books for his mother, too.

At the library, he went to the children's area. Nobody else was there, and he sat on the floor near a bookcase of easy readers. They might be all right, he thought. He remembered that there weren't too many words on each page. He opened one, looking at pictures of animals dressed up in clothes and acting like people. It wasn't for grown-ups. He felt silly just looking at it.

"Why are you reading that?"

Joseph looked up. Mark was standing there. "It's not for me. It's for . . ." He paused. "What difference does it make?"

"No difference, I guess." Then Mark said, "I followed you here."

"You followed me? Why?"

"I didn't think you wanted to walk with me. Every time I want to do something with you,

you say you're busy." Mark sat down on one of the small chairs. "Why are you mad at me?"

Joseph looked away. "I'm not mad at you. Did you follow me here to ask me that?"

"No. I came here to get some money from my mother so I could go to the pet store and get a bell collar for our cat. He brought another bird inside this morning through the pet door and left it under the kitchen table. My mother had a fit. She told me she wanted Tony to have the collar on when she got home. Anyway, I forgot to take the money from her before I went to school."

Joseph looked around. "Where is she?" There was one lady at the checkout counter and another shelving books. Two men were reading at the tables in the adult section.

"She's downstairs in the meeting room. She helps the adult-literacy teacher on Wednesday afternoons."

"Adult literacy? Is that a class for grown-ups who don't read already?"

"Yes." Mark stood up. "I won't bother you anymore." He started walking away.

"Wait," Joseph said, too loudly. Then he

lowered his voice. "Come back a minute." He couldn't keep it to himself any longer.

Joseph motioned him to sit down. "I'm going to tell you why I've been staying away from you."

"It's about time," Mark said.

"It's okay if you don't want to be friends after this."

"Will you just tell me what's going on?"

"My mother can't read," Joseph said, and without stopping he told Mark everything about his mother getting lost and how he was trying to teach her to read.

"It's like you're the parent," Mark said.

Joseph looked at him, surprised. "I never thought about it like that. Maybe that's why I don't want to help her anymore. I don't want to be a parent yet. Sometimes I don't even like being the oldest kid."

"Being the youngest isn't always so great, either," Mark said. "Why didn't you tell me this before?"

"I thought you'd make fun of my family. Your father's a college professor and your mother—"

"She embarrasses me sometimes. She can be really whacko."

They both laughed. Then Joseph said, "Do you think my mother could go to the class here?"

"Let's see."

Joseph followed Mark down some stairs he had never noticed before. The door to a big room on the lower level was open, but they stayed in the hall just out of sight.

"There are twelve people who come when my mother is here," Mark said. "It's free. Some can't speak English very well yet. My mother remembers what that was like. Maybe they just came to the United States. The others didn't learn to read well when they were young. There are usually two tutors who work along with the teacher. My mother loves helping. She says everybody who comes to class really wants to learn, not like in regular school."

Just then, Mark's mother came out into the hall. "I thought I heard you. Joseph! I haven't seen you in a while."

"Do you want to tell her, or should I?" Mark said.

"I'll tell her."

Mark's mother listened without interrupting him. When Joseph had finished, he asked, "Do you think my mother could be in this class?"

"Wouldn't it be better if she came in the morning? You have a little brother, don't you, who goes to kindergarten then?"

"I didn't think about that." Mark's mother hadn't acted shocked at all about his mother not reading.

"Have her come tomorrow if she wants. She doesn't have to wait any longer."

"She doesn't really want to come," Joseph said. "She thinks she'll have trouble."

"A lot of people feel that way at first. Tell her that, Joseph. Then they discover they can really learn. Things aren't the same for them now as when they were young. Besides, it isn't your responsibility to teach your mother. You've done much more than you had to. Would you like me to talk to her? Would that help?"

Joseph shook his head. "I'll do it."

"I have to go back in now," she said. "I'm glad you came by."

"Wait." Mark stood in her way. "I need the

money for Tony's bell collar. I forgot to take it this morning."

On the way upstairs, Joseph said, "I'll go to the pet store with you if you'll stop at my house first. My mother will worry if I'm too late getting home. She was going to make cookies today, too."

"Let's go," Mark said. "Your mother is the best cook in the world."

Seven

After Jen and Peter had gone to bed that night, Joseph told his mother about the literacy class. "They had books and there were small groups working with a teacher or tutor."

She looked worried. "Maybe I wouldn't fit into one of the groups."

"Why wouldn't you fit in? Everybody there looked happy. It wasn't quiet like in regular school. They were talking and laughing. Mark's mother said at first you might worry about learning to read now, but after you get started, you'll see you can do it."

"I know I can do it here, Joseph. Did you bring books home from the library for me?"

"No!" Joseph said firmly. "I'll help you if you have trouble with words, but somebody else will have to teach you to begin with. You're not my kid."

He ran out the kitchen door, onto the roof. Without a jacket, he began to shiver, and walked back and forth so that the cold October night air wouldn't chill him too much. He looked up the hill, away from the bright lights along Fourth Street. What kinds of problems did people in houses up there have, he wondered. For sure they knew how to read. Well, maybe not all of them did. Nobody had it perfect, no matter who they were or where they lived.

Just then Joseph felt a jacket rest around his shoulders. His mother had come out without his hearing her. She stood next to him, wrapping her arms around herself. "You're right, Joseph. I have to learn from someone else. It's not fair to you. You've done so much already."

He didn't answer.

"Tomorrow I'll go to the library."

Joseph put his arms into the jacket and zipped it up. "Mark's mother said they have a class in the morning, so you can be there while Peter is in school."

The next morning, everyone but his father was getting ready to leave. Joseph sat down next to him at the table and put some bread into the toaster. Then Jen came in. "Mommy's getting ready to go to school," she said. They heard the hair dryer go on in the bathroom and smiled at one another. It was okay that she wasn't there helping them.

"You saw the class, Joseph," his father said. "Do you really think it will be good for her?"

"Mark's mother thinks so."

"I'm going to walk with her," Jen said. "Then I won't have to be alone with Peter." She turned in her chair. "Where is he? Hurry up, Peter, or we'll be late," she called.

Just then Joseph's mother came in. "Do I look all right?"

"You're beautiful," Joseph's father said. "Sit down and eat."

"I'm not really hungry. Jen, go check on Peter."

"You have to eat something," Joseph said. "That's what you always tell us."

They all laughed

As soon as Joseph got to school, he told Mark that his mother had decided to go to the literacy class.

Mark was glad. "My mom wanted me to tell you," he said, "that if something isn't right, she'll see if she can straighten it out."

Joseph thought about his mother all day. When he got home, she was sitting at the table with an open workbook in front of her. She smiled at him. "We call the teacher by her first name—Nora. She wore jeans, too."

"What did you do?" Joseph asked, sitting down opposite her.

"Take off your jacket. There's time."

"Well, tell me," he said, unzipping it automatically.

"First she asked me questions and filled out a form about me."

"What kinds of questions?"

"How old I was, if I was married, how long I went to school, why I wanted to come to class."

"What did you say?"

"Joseph, I said I wanted to learn to read. She didn't even ask me why I didn't know how. She was nice. Then I had a little test with a tutor. It showed them I know my letters and I understand directions."

"Did you learn anything new?"

"Wait, I forgot to say something." She smiled. "They introduced me to everyone in the class and they each said something nice like they were glad I was there. Some of them had trouble saying it in English because they're just learning to speak it. Nora said we all help each other."

"So you like it?"

Joseph's mother nodded.

Just then Jen came in from school. "Her teacher's name is Nora," Joseph said.

Jen looked surprised. "You call her by her first name? That's really weird."

Joseph and his mother laughed.

"What's this book you brought home?" he asked, picking it up and turning the pages.

"Nora said we'd do everything in class, but if we wanted to we could take a workbook home and do extra pages." Then she opened a new notebook. "We also copied a little story that we made up and that Nora wrote on the board. See?"

"Do you know what it says?" Joseph asked.

"A few of the words. Nora said to be patient.

It will take a long time to read really well, but she thinks I'll be able to do it."

"What does she mean by a long time?" Joseph asked.

"I don't know, but if I keep getting better, it doesn't matter."

Two months later, what did matter, Joseph thought as he walked home from school, was that his mother was still going to class. Not that day. On Fridays there wasn't any. But on the other days of the week, she left with them in the morning. In the evening she sat at the kitchen table and practiced something she had learned that day, while Joseph worked on his Target assignments.

By then the bridge was all fixed. No more detours.

As Joseph walked along, he felt a few snow-flakes touch his face. In December that was no surprise. Some kids in school had said at least a foot would fall that day. Mark had been talking about skiing for a couple of weeks already. Last year Joseph had gone once with Mark's family. It was after a big snowfall, when he had made a lot of money shoveling. Skiing was fun, but too expensive to do very often.

The next morning he and Mark were going to the college gym to swim and use the exercise equipment. It was free for faculty kids, and they could bring a guest on Saturday mornings. Once soccer had ended, they started going there.

By the time Joseph got home, the snow was beginning to stick. He hopped to the back door, leaving footprints from only one foot. He wondered if Jen would notice.

Inside, he was surprised to see his father. "Why aren't you at work?"

"They cancelled my shift because we're going to get a big blizzard. It's coming from the west."

"I thought the kids in school were making that up."

"No, it's coming." He had been holding a piece of paper. With a worried look on his face, he handed it to Joseph. "Your mother told me she was going shopping and Peter would stay with Mrs. Rivera after school so I could sleep. But when I woke up I found that note."

"Mom wrote it?" Joseph said, and read it out

loud. " 'I went to the Valley Mall by bus. I will be back by 3.' " He looked at the clock, then at his father. "It's three-thirty now."

Jen opened the back door and let her book bag drop to the floor. "Go get Peter," his father said to her. "He's with Mrs. Rivera." Then he turned back to Joseph. "I thought she was just going to shop around here. She had to transfer from one bus to another to get there. She's never done it alone."

Joseph thought about what had happened when she took the bus to the employment agency. He looked at the note again. "How do you spell *valley*?"

"She spelled it right," his father answered. "If she's not home by four—"

Just then the door opened again. Joseph's mother stepped onto the mat and started stamping the snow off her shoes. She held out two large shopping bags full of boxes. "Here, take them," she said. Then she smiled. "Don't just stand there and stare. The snow made the bus a little late." They reached quickly for the bags. "You shouldn't have worried. I knew what to do." She took off her coat and shoes. "Put the bags in the bedroom and don't peek."

By the time they were back in the kitchen, Jen had come in with Peter.

"Everyone, sit down," Joseph's mother said. "I'll make cocoa." She filled the kettle with water and turned on the heat. Then she took something from her purse and sat down, too.

"What's that?" Peter asked.

"A bus schedule. This week in class we learned to read it." She opened it up so they could all see the map. "We learned the street names on the route and the names of the main stops."

"You had to transfer at Gateway Mall to get to Valley Mall," Joseph's father said.

She smiled. "It was easy. I could read the signs, and I knew when the bus was supposed to come." She turned the schedule over. "See, Joseph, here's the timetable on this side."

"There are so many numbers," he said.

She laughed. "I'll help you figure it out."

"I thought you were going to shop around here," his father said.

The water started boiling. She got mugs and mixed the cocoa. "This week Nora had us

looking at ads because it's so close to the holidays. There were some good sales at the Mall, so we made lists of what we wanted to buy at different stores."

Joseph listened. Two months ago, this couldn't have happened the way it had. Wait till he told Mark. After he had his cocoa, he said, "I'm going out on the roof. There's enough snow to make snowballs."

His sister and brother went out, too.

Joseph looked down at Fourth Street. The lights were already on, making the snow look yellow from a distance. Suddenly a snowball hit him on the back. He scooped up some snow fast and turned around. "I'll get you," he shouted, tossing it at Jen.

She slipped and fell, then turned over. "I'm going to make a snow angel." Peter was off by himself, pushing snow into a pile in one corner.

Joseph looked toward the kitchen window. His parents were still talking, holding hands. He scooped up some more snow and rounded it perfectly. It was just sticky enough. Maybe the next day, instead of going to the gym, he and Mark would go sledding in Mountain Park.

Joseph took the snowball he had just made and threw it as far as he could, up the hill into the middle of the street. He made some more, then threw them, too, trying to reach farther and farther.